A Note to Parents and Caregivers:

Read-it! Joke Books are for children who are moving ahead on the amazing road to reading. These fun books support the acquisition and extension of reading skills as well as a love of books.

Published by the same company that produces *Read-it!* Readers, these books introduce the question/answer and dialogue patterns that help children expand their thinking about language structure and book formats.

When sharing joke books with a child, read in short stretches. Pause often to talk about the meaning of the jokes. The question/answer and dialogue formats work well for this purpose and provide an opportunity to talk about the language and meaning of the jokes. Have the child turn the pages and point to the pictures and familiar words. When you read the jokes, have fun creating the voices of characters or emphasizing some important words. Be sure to reread favorite jokes.

There is no right or wrong way to share books with children. Find time to read with your child, and pass on the legacy of literacy.

Adria F. Klein, Ph.D.
Professor Emeritus
California State University
San Bernardino, California

Editor: Christianne Jones
Designer: Joe Anderson
Creative Director: Keith Griffin
Editorial Director: Carol Jones
Managing Editor: Catherine Neitge
The illustrations in this book were created digitally.

Picture Window Books
5115 Excelsior Boulevard
Suite 232
Minneapolis, MN 55416
877-845-8392
www.picturewindowbooks.com

Printed in the United States of America.

Library of Congress Cataloging-in-Publication Data
Ziegler, Mark, 1954-
Nutty names : a book of name jokes / by Mark Ziegler ; illustrated by
Ryan Haugen.
p. cm. – (Read-it! joke books--supercharged!)
ISBN 1-4048-1163-X (hardcover)
1. Names, Personal–Juvenile humor. I. Haugen, Ryan, 1972- II. Title.
III. Series.

PN6231.N24Z54 2006
818'.602–dc22
2005004071

NUTTY NAMES

A Book of Name Jokes

by Mark Ziegler   illustrated by Ryan Haugen

Special thanks to our advisers for their expertise:

Adria F. Klein, Ph.D.
Professor Emeritus, California State University
San Bernardino, California

Susan Kesselring, M.A.
Literacy Educator
Rosemount–Apple Valley–Eagan (Minnesota) School District

PICTURE WINDOW BOOKS
Minneapolis, Minnesota

**What do you call a
girl who wears
just one shoe?**
Eileen.

**What do you call a boy
who floats in the water?**
Bob.

What do you call a boy who
sleeps by the front door?
Matt.

What do you call a girl
who scoops up fish?
Annette.

What do you call a girl who stands with a foot on each side of the river?
Bridget.

What do you call a guy who puts water in a hole?
Phil.

**What do you call
a camel with
no humps?**
Humphrey.

**What do you call a guy who
stands in a deep hole?**
Doug.

**What do you call a boy
who sits in a bowl?**
Stu.

What do you call a boy who hangs on a museum wall?

Art.

What do you call a girl who has a frog on her head?

Lily.

**What do you call a guy who
picks up an angry cat?**
Claude.

**What do you call a girl
standing in the distance?**
Dot.

What do you call a girl who
holds coats in the hallway?
Peg.

What do you call a boy who
lifts a car with his head?
Jack.

What do you call a boy who plays in a pile of leaves?
Russell.

What do you call a girl who lives on the beach?
Sandy.

What do you call a guy who has one foot in the door?
Justin.

What do you call a boy who lays on the grass each morning?
Dewey.

What do you call a boy who has a seagull nesting on his head?
Cliff.

What do you call a boy who is covered in fur?
Harry.

**What do you call a boy who
acts like a real hot dog?**
  Frank.

**What do you call a girl who
climbs up the side of a house?**
  Ivy.

**What do you call a boy
who is always crying?**
  Waylen.

**What do you call a boy
who likes to workout?**
  Jim.

**What do you call a guy
who owes money?**
  Bill.

**What do you call a girl
who sits on a pizza?**
Olive.

**What do you call a boy
who is half eaten by
a snake?**
Les.

What do you call a girl who sits in a Halloween bag?
Candy.

What do you call a boy who likes putting numbers together?
Adam.

What do you call a girl who always thinks of other people's feelings?
Karen.

What do you call a girl who steals things?
Robin.

What do you call a boy who scribbles pictures all over the wall?
Drew.

What do you call a pesky girl who buzzes around your head?
Nat.

What do you call a girl who sits on a hamburger bun?
Patty.

What do you call a boy who's a bit of sunshine?
Ray.

**What do you call a boy
who is always first?**
Juan.

**What do you call a boy who
hides stuff in the ground?**
Barry.

What do you call a girl who
comes around every summer?
  June.

What do you call a boy
who has eight arms?
  Hans.

What do you call a girl who babbles in the middle of a field?
Brook.

What do you call a guy who can breathe under water?
Gil.

Read-it! Joke Books— Supercharged!

Beastly Laughs: A Book of Monster Jokes by Michael Dahl

Chalkboard Chuckles: A Book of Classroom Jokes by Mark Moore

Chitchat Chuckles: A Book of Funny Talk by Mark Ziegler

Creepy Crawlers: A Book of Bug Jokes by Mark Moore

Critter Jitters: A Book of Animal Jokes by Mark Ziegler

Fur, Feathers, and Fun! A Book of Animal Jokes by Mark Ziegler

Giggle Bubbles: A Book of Underwater Jokes by Mark Ziegler

Goofballs! A Book of Sports Jokes by Mark Ziegler

Lunchbox Laughs: A Book of Food Jokes by Mark Ziegler

Mind Knots: A Book of Riddles by Mark Ziegler

Roaring with Laughter: A Book of Animal Jokes by Michael Dahl

School Kidders: A Book of School Jokes by Mark Ziegler

Sit! Stay! Laugh! A Book of Pet Jokes by Michael Dahl

Spooky Sillies: A Book of Ghost Jokes by Mark Moore

Wacky Wheelies: A Book of Transportation Jokes by Mark Ziegler

Wacky Workers: A Book of Job Jokes by Mark Ziegler

What's up, Doc? A Book of Doctor Jokes by Mark Ziegler

Looking for a specific title or level? A complete list of *Read-it!* Readers is available on our Web site: **www.picturewindowbooks.com**